This book belongs to:

_____

For Chris,
who only saw the
first draft and loved it.

American edition published in 2020 by Andersen Press USA,
an imprint of Andersen Press Ltd.
www.andersenpressusa.com

First published in Great Britain in 2020 by Andersen Press Ltd.,
20 Vauxhall Bridge Road, London SWIV 2SA.

Distributed in the United States and Canada by
Lerner Publishing Group, Inc.
241 First Avenue North
Minneapolis, MN 55401 USA

For reading levels and more information, look up this title at www.lernerbooks.com.

Library of Congress Cataloging-in-Publication Data Available
ISBN: 978 1 72842 4118

I - TOPPAN LEFUNG - 9/2020

A ~~Rabbit~~ Fox Called Herbert

MARGARET STURTON

Andersen Press USA

Herbert loved foxes.

Herbert loved foxes so much, he made himself a pair of red ears.

"Rabbit ears aren't short and pointy," laughed
Herbert's mummy. Reluctantly, Herbert let
his ears look rabbity again.

The next day, Herbert painted himself red with the help of his little sister.

Then they played find-the-fox.

Herbert's mummy was cross.
"Look at the mess you've made!" she said.
"Promise me you will be a good rabbit."

Herbert helped to clean up.

A few days later, Herbert made himself a lovely new tail. He and his little sister played chase-a-tail until Mummy came to see what was happening.

"Cutting up my favorite dress was very naughty," scolded Herbert's mummy. "Promise me you will be a good rabbit."

Herbert said nothing.

Then one day when he was allowed out to play, Herbert did all the things he wasn't supposed to do.

He didn't try to be a good rabbit.

"Look, Mummy," said Herbert's little sister. "Look at Herbert."

"Herbert, come here, right away!"
called Herbert's mummy.

"I don't understand," said Herbert's mummy. "Why are you dressed like that when I asked you to be a good rabbit?"

"I CAN'T be a good rabbit!" said Herbert.
"Why not?" asked his mummy.
"Because . . ." said Herbert:

I AM
A FOX!

Herbert's mummy said
nothing as they looked
at each other.

Until at last, she said,
"Oh Herbert . . .

Yes. You are my fox."